Dream Dogs

SASHA

D0373913

With special thanks to Lucy Courtenay and Nellie Ryan

First published in Great Britain by HarperCollins *Children's Books* 2010
HarperCollins Children's Books is a division of HarperCollins*Publishers* Ltd,
77-85 Fulham Palace Road, Hammersmith, London W6 8JB

The HarperCollins *Children's Books* website address is
www.harpercollins.co.uk

2

Dream Dogs : Sasha
Text copyright © HarperCollins 2010
Illustrations copyright © HarperCollins 2010

ISBN-13 978 0 00 732035 6

Printed and bound in England by
Clays Ltd, St Ives plc

Conditions of Sale
This book is sold subject to the condition that it shall not, by way of trade
or otherwise, be lent, re-sold, hired out or otherwise circulated without the
publisher's prior written consent in any form of binding or cover other than
that in which it is published and without a similar condition including this
condition being imposed on the subsequent purchaser.

Mixed Sources
Product group from well-managed
forests and other controlled sources
www.fsc.org Cert no. SW-COC-1806
© 1996 Forest Stewardship Council

FSC is a non-profit international organisation established to promote the
responsible management of the world's forests. Products carrying the FSC
label are independently certified to assure consumers that they come
from forests that are managed to meet the social, economic and
ecological needs of present and future generations.

Find out more about HarperCollins and the environment at
www.harpercollins.co.uk/green

SASHA

Aimee Harper

HarperCollins *Children's Books*

Special thanks to
The Happy Dog Grooming Parlour, Farnham

Introducing...

Name: Sasha

Breed: Bichon frise

Age: 4

Colour: White when freshly shampooed

Likes: Bows, kisses, being pampered, winning rosettes

Dislikes: Hairdryers, muddy puddles, Silky

Most likely to be mistaken for: A cotton wool ball

Party trick: Licking people's noses!

One

The Show's Tonight!

The sand crunched under Bella's school shoes, and the salty air blew through her hair. Even though she had lived in Sandmouth for a month now, Bella still felt a thrill whenever they went to the beach. And as the beach was on the way to and from school, Bella walked along it twice a day.

It was a bright, clear afternoon. Staring up
at the seagulls in the blue sky, Bella was caught
by surprise when a sand ball hit her on the
back of her coat.

"Hey!" Bella shouted. She swung round.
"Louie, don't!"

Louie stuck out his tongue and aimed at Bella with his second sand ball. Bella looked over her little brother's shoulder and grinned. A tall girl with blonde plaits was creeping up on Louie. In her hand was the biggest sand ball Bella had ever seen.

"Get him, Amber!" Bella shouted.

She cheered as her best friend Amber dumped the sand ball down the back of Louie's neck.

"That's not fair!" Louie complained, wriggling and laughing.

"Course it's fair," Amber said. "There aren't any rules in a sand-ball fight."

Louie threw his second sand ball at Amber. It missed.

"Tough luck, Louie!" Bella called as Amber caught up with her.

Louie shrugged, grinning. He ran down to the edge of the sea to kick at the waves.

"I still can't believe you called your dog Snowy," said Bella as they watched Amber's jet-black spaniel splashing through the waves with Louie and Amber's brother Joe.

"That's me!" Amber grinned. She pulled a silly face. "Crazee!"

Snowy plunged into the sea, soaking Louie and Joe. Their shouts floated up the beach towards Bella.

"Snowy really needs a wash," Amber said, linking arms with Bella. "He's been in the sea so much lately that his coat feels like a doormat."

"Mum loves it when the dogs get really dirty," Bella said. "It's really satisfying, she says, seeing all the muck going down the plughole."

Bella's mum Suzi had been rushed off her feet ever since opening her new dog parlour, Dream

11

Dogs. Bella had lost count of the different kinds

of dogs they'd washed. Big ones, tiny ones,

hairy ones and ones with hardly any coat at all,

puppies and old ones and licky ones and growly

ones. Bella's dog Pepper was used to it now,

but for the first week he'd spent the whole time

barking at the customers.

"It's great that your mum can fit in Snowy

today," Amber said. "I know she's busy."

Bella nodded. "Mum's booked eight dogs in

to Dream Dogs today," she said. "She usually

does four!"

"Because of the Sandmouth Dog Show?"

Amber guessed.

The annual dog show took place on the last

Friday in February every year. It was held in the town hall, and had categories for everything, from proper pedigree dog competitions to funny classes for dogs that looked like their owners, or had the waggiest tale.

"Yes," Bella said. "I think everyone in Sandmouth is entering."

"Including Snowy," Amber agreed.

Bella and Amber both looked at the soggy spaniel as he galloped along the beach.

"It's hard to believe Snowy's a pedigree, isn't it?" said Amber.

"It's hard to believe he's a *dog*," Bella giggled. "He looks more like a sand monster. He needs a *lot* of work to get him ready for the show tonight."

They climbed the steps up to the road. Louie and Joe jogged up after them, followed by Snowy and Amber's mum Claire. Claire was tall and slim, and her short spiky hair was the same colour as Amber's.

"It's a big help that Amber and Joe can stay for tea with you today," Claire said. "I've got so much to do for Snowy's class. The extra couple of hours will be a real help. Sometimes I think this dog show's more trouble than it's

worth."

"You don't mean that, Mum," said Amber.

"You love showing Snowy off."

"We'll bring Amber and Joe to the show,"

said Bella. "We're coming anyway. Mum

entered Pepper in the Most Obedient Dog

class."

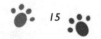

Amber burst out laughing. "But Pepper isn't obedient!" she said. "He hardly ever does what your mum tells him!"

"I know," Bella sighed. "But he isn't a pedigree, and the Obedience class was the only group which had any space left. As usual, my mum left it till the last minute."

Bella's dog Pepper was small and brown and very cute. But obedience really wasn't his thing. Bella felt nervous as she thought about tonight's show.

Would Pepper behave himself?

Or were they in for the most embarrassing evening of their lives?

Two

Busy Busy Busy

They turned into Bella's road. The bright pink

Dream Dogs sign winked and shone at them

above Dream Dogs' window. With its

bubblegum-coloured walls, grass-coloured floor

and hanging plants, the parlour looked warm

and inviting. Bella felt her tummy bubble with

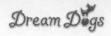

joy. She loved Dream Dogs so much. It had

been hard work making it perfect, but now it

looked as gorgeous as a birthday cake.

Bella pushed open the door. Pepper dropped

the smelly bone he had been chewing and

leaped out of his basket. He jumped up at Bella

and Louie like he hadn't seen them for days.

"Good day, kids?" Suzi said, straightening up from the parlour's special dog bath which was raised up on a platform.

"Fine," said Bella, Louie, Joe and Amber all together.

"Thanks for picking up Bella and Louie, Claire," said Suzi, turning to Amber's mum. "I've been run off my feet today."

A very soggy white West Highland terrier scrambled out of the bath and shook himself. Suzi caught the drops in a towel.

"Only two more to go," she said as she rubbed the little Westie. "No offence to Snowy, Claire, but I'll be pleased when today is over!"

"Mum?" said Bella hopefully. "Have you been

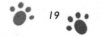

practising the obedience stuff with Pepper

today?"

Pepper started jumping madly all over

Snowy.

"Down, Pepper!" Suzi ordered, wiping her

forehead and leaving behind a trail of soapsuds.

Pepper took no notice.

"I guess not," Bella sighed.

"Give me a hand, will you, girls?" asked Suzi.

She waved two towels at Bella and Amber. "Time's moving on. I need to make a start on Snowy."

Amber cheered and threw her school bag down in the corner. She loved drying the dogs, especially when they used the big dog-dryer. Pepper had hated that dryer for the first two weeks. Now he was used to it, and just sighed and stuck his nose under the woolly blanket in his basket.

Bella and Amber dried the Westie, and Louie took Joe upstairs to the flat to see his monster collection. The two mums chatted about the Sandmouth Dog Show as Pepper went back to his bone.

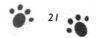

"You wouldn't believe how seriously some people take it," Claire said. "I don't usually go to dog shows with Snowy, but I do this one because it's local. It's supposed to be a bit of fun. But some of the other dog owners... Well!"

"I know what you mean," Suzi agreed. She tested the temperature of the water in the shower attachment. "One lady wanted to book the last available slot before the dog show to make sure her dog was groomed as close to the judging as possible. She was ever so fussy about it."

"What kind of dog, Mum?" Bella asked, still towelling the Westie.

"A bichon frise," said her mum, smiling.

"Oh!" Bella gasped, picturing a little fluffy white bichon frise dog. "They are just so cute!"

"I know!" Suzi agreed. "Their fur is so soft and curly. They're like little teddy bears."

Claire frowned. "Who's the owner?" she said.

"Mrs Lockett, she said her name was," said Suzi.

23

Claire started laughing. "Look out for Helen Lockett!" she said. "She's terrible!"

"Mr Boswell is worse," Amber pointed out.

"Brian Boswell has a bichon frise as well," Claire explained as Bella and Suzi looked puzzled. "He and Mrs Lockett are arch-enemies. Especially during the Sandmouth Dog Show."

"Thank goodness he hasn't booked an appointment, then," Suzi said.

The parlour's phone rang. Bella left Amber with the Westie.

"Hello, Dream Dogs," she said into the receiver.

"I need an appointment for my dog this

evening," snapped a voice.

"I'm afraid we haven't
got an appointment—"
Bella began.

"You'll have to find one,"
said the voice. "It's most

important. My usual salon has let me down at

the last minute, and I'm entered in the

Sandmouth Dog Show. I usually win, by the

way. I am also *very* influential with Sandmouth's

dog owners. If you don't find me an appointment,

then you will be making a big mistake."

Bella covered the receiver. "There's a

grumpy man on the phone who wants an

appointment tonight, Mum," she said.

Suzi had just got Snowy up the steps and into the bath. She groaned. "Take his name, and I'll try to fit him in," she said.

"That'll be *nine* dogs today, Mum!" Bella gasped. "That's more than twice as many as normal!"

"Dream Dogs is a new business," Suzi said firmly. "I can't turn anyone down."

Bella took her hand off the receiver. "What's your name, please?" she asked.

"Boswell," said the voice. "Brian Boswell."

Bella's heart fluttered. It was the other bichon frise owner. The one Claire and Amber had just warned them about!

"Um," she said nervously. "We'll do our best.

But I really don't think—"

"I'll bring my dog in at six o'clock," Brian Boswell interrupted. "It can be your last appointment of the day. I'll make it worth your while. Goodbye."

The receiver buzzed in Bella's ear as Brian Boswell hung up. Bella stared at it. He hadn't left his number, so her mum couldn't call him back. Bella checked the phone's screen. *Number withheld*.

The last appointment? Mrs Lockett had asked for the last appointment. And Mrs Lockett was booked in at five. Bella had a *really* bad feeling about this!

Three

Mrs Lockett

The West Highland terrier's owner was an elderly lady called Miss Waldicott. Miss Waldicott was delighted when she came to collect her dog.

"You've done a lovely job with Angus, Suzi, dear," she said to Bella's mum.

"Thanks, Miss Waldicott," said Suzi, raising her voice over the noise of the dryer as she worked on Snowy. "Bella and Amber dried him for you. I've never been so busy!"

Miss Waldicott patted her Westie on the head. "Will you be at the show tonight?" she asked Bella.

"We've entered Pepper in the Obedience class," Bella said.

"I've entered Angus for that as well," Miss Waldicott said, sounding pleased. "He's such a good little fellow. Aren't you, Angus? Show the nice people how you shake my hand."

The Westie sat obediently and lifted his little white paw into the air.

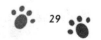 29

"Aah," said Amber as Miss Waldicott gave her dog a little treat.

Bella smiled bravely. Pepper didn't do that. Pepper didn't do anything you told him, really. He just liked to cuddle her by wrapping his paws round her neck. And chase white vans. She had a feeling they wouldn't count.

Miss Waldicott pressed two fifty pence pieces into Bella and Amber's hands. "For your help, dears," she said. "See you later."

As the door swung shut behind Miss Waldicott, Suzi turned off the big dryer. Amber's dog Snowy looked magnificent. His coat shone and his ears were neatly trimmed. Bella could hardly believe he was the same dog she'd seen on the beach only an hour earlier.

"Sorry I've rushed Snowy, Claire," Suzi said.

"But now I have to fit Mr Boswell in..."

"Snowy looks great," said Claire warmly.

"But I still think you're crazy to take on Mr

Boswell. I wouldn't like to be in your shoes if

Mrs Lockett finds out."

The salon door tinkled. Bella turned and saw a very glamorous lady in a beige linen jumpsuit standing in the door. A fluffy white bundle lay in her arms. Bella's heart melted. Bichon frises were *gorgeous*.

"Mrs Lockett?" said Suzi brightly. "Please come in. And this must be Sasha."

Bella fixed her eyes on Sasha, the bichon frise. Sasha gazed back with bright black button eyes.

"Hello, Helen," said Claire politely.

"Claire," said Mrs Lockett with a nod of her head. "Still got your little spaniel, I see?"

"Snowy's not little," Amber said indignantly. "He's quite big for his breed."

Mrs Lockett ignored Amber. She took Sasha's collar and lead off and hung them on one of the hooks by the door. Then she gave Sasha to Suzi, with a long list of instructions.

"Sasha's skin is very sensitive... I hope you use only the very best products... you must never comb her through when her fur is still wet because it breaks..."

Bella glanced at Amber, who rolled her eyes.

Mrs Lockett was talking to Suzi as if Bella's mum had never washed a dog before.

"... whatever you do, don't direct the dryer inside her ears, it drives her quite mad... I'll be back to collect her at five forty-five."

With a swirl of expensive perfume, Mrs Lockett left the shop. But not before she'd given Pepper a snooty look.

"Funny little dog," she said. "A mongrel, I suppose. Oh well."

"Well!" said Bella furiously as the salon door swung shut behind Mrs Lockett. "What a rude lady!"

"She's nothing compared to Mr Boswell," said Claire.

Suzi brought Sasha
up to her face.
"Aren't you
lovely!" she cooed.
"Now, into the
bath. We haven't got
long." Sasha put out a small
pink tongue and licked Suzi's nose.

Bella tore her eyes from the little dog. She
knew she was grinning like a twit. A bichon
frise was very hard to resist.

Suzi turned on the shower head and started
gently wetting Sasha's curly white fur. "Bella,
why don't you take Amber upstairs?" she
suggested. "I made a big plate of sandwiches

35

for tea. I just hope Louie and Joe have left some for you girls!"

Claire checked her watch. "I have to go," she said. "Thanks again, Suzi. Tell Joe I'll see him later. Bye Amber, love. Be good."

Amber kissed her mum and Snowy goodbye. Then she followed Bella and Pepper up to the flat. Joe and Louie had already started on the sandwiches, and were in the middle of an argument about which flavour crisps were best.

At five forty-five, Louie and Joe went back to Louie's monster collection. Leaving Pepper snoozing on Bella's bed, the girls headed down to see how Suzi was getting on with Sasha.

"Mum, she looks even *more* gorgeous!" said

Bella, clapping her hands.

Sasha stood on the drying table Suzi used for small dogs. She waved her little pompom tail. Her coat had been fluffed up into a perfect white ball. As Bella put her fingers into Sasha's fur, it was like putting her hand into cotton wool.

"With a dog like this, you can't go wrong," Suzi said proudly. "Fetch her collar and lead for me, will you, Bella? Mrs Lockett will be back at any moment."

Bella went over to the hooks. Halfway there, she stopped dead and stared out of the window. A large man in a custard-coloured jacket was striding down the street. In his arms was a white, fluffy bundle.

It could only be one person.

"Mum, it's Mr Boswell!" Bella squealed. "*He's early!*"

Four

Oops!

Suzi went pale. "Oh dear!" she gulped. "Didn't
Claire say Mr Boswell would be difficult if he
knew I was doing Mrs Lockett's dog as well as
his? Mrs Lockett is due at any minute! They'll
see each other!"

"I'll take Sasha up to the flat," Amber

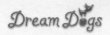

suggested at once.

"Quickly!" Bella begged. Mr Boswell was almost at the door of the salon. She prayed he wouldn't look up and see his rival's dog through the big glass window.

Amber scooped Sasha under her arm and ran. The adjoining door to the flat swung shut just as Mr Boswell reached Dream Dogs. His large red face peered through the parlour window. Bella saw him wrinkle his nose. Then he pushed open the door.

"Very *pink*, aren't you?" Brian Boswell said disapprovingly, gazing around the parlour.

"The dogs like it, Mr Boswell," Suzi said with a big smile.

Mr Boswell's bichon frise blinked at Bella from the crook of his arm as he paced up and down the salon. "Very small too," he grumbled, glancing around. "Hardly room to swing a Chihuahua." He stroked his little bichon frise's head. His dog looked so perfect that it was hard to believe she hadn't been washed or trimmed yet.

"Well, beggars can't be choosers," said Mr

41

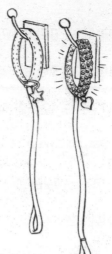

Boswell at last, removing his dog's collar and lead and hanging them up beside Sasha's. "Now, Silky has a very particular washing routine..."

And Mr Boswell was off on a list of instructions that sounded even more complicated than Mrs Lockett's. Bella stood by the door, staring out into the street. She bit her lip anxiously. This was SERIOUS. Mrs Lockett would come to collect Sasha at any minute. And her mum would lose two clients in one go!

"Fine, fine!" Suzi was saying. She ushered Mr Boswell to the door. "Leave her with me. I'm sure you have some important last-minute things to do before tonight's big show. Silky will be ready to collect in forty minutes!"

Mr Boswell left the salon reluctantly. When he had disappeared, Suzi slumped against the wall. She covered her face with her hands.

"That was close!" she said faintly. "Any sign of Mrs Lockett yet, Bella?"

"Coming the other way," Bella giggled. "She hasn't seen Mr Boswell. I reckon we've got two minutes. Mum! I can't believe—"

"Take Silky to Amber and bring Sasha back in!" Suzi interrupted, straightening her apron. "With any luck, we'll get away with this. But you have to be *quick*!"

Bella picked up Silky. The dog was as light as a feather. Then she opened the door that led to the flat's staircase. Amber was hiding in the hallway with Sasha. Bella felt Silky stiffen.

"Wrow!" barked Silky in a little high voice. "Wrow! Wrow!"

"Wrow!" Sasha barked back.

"Shh!" Bella hissed helplessly. Mrs Lockett would hear!

Sasha was now growling too. The two dogs obviously hated each other.

"Oh!" Amber squealed as Sasha wriggled out of her grasp and jumped to the floor.

The sight of her enemy gave Silky extra strength. She pushed herself out of Bella's arms

and jumped down as well. Sasha and Silky
started running round each other, nipping at
each other's legs and growling squeakily.

"Um, Bella?" said Amber in a strange voice.
"Which dog is which?"

Bella stared at the two bichon frises. Neither of them had their collars on. Both of them were girls. Both of them were white and fluffy... and *completely identical*.

"I don't know," said Bella in dismay.

She looked from one dog to the other, and back again. The more she looked, the more confused she felt.

"Oh no!" Amber squealed. "What are we going to do?"

Bella had an idea. She bent over Silky / Sasha and sniffed her.

"This one's Sasha," she said in relief. "Her head smells of the lavender shampoo Mum used."

Amber picked up Silky just as Suzi put her head round the door. "What's the delay, girls?" she said urgently. "Mrs Lockett is nearly at the door!"

"Here's Sasha, Mum!" said Bella, scooping up the little dog and dashing back into the salon.

Ting-a-ling-a-ling.

"Finished?" asked Mrs Lockett, closing the Dream Dogs' door.

Bella's mum looked a bit trembly. "Of course, Mrs Lockett," she said, swallowing. "We try not to let our clients down at Dream Dogs."

Mrs Lockett walked round Sasha twice. She felt her ears. She stroked her coat. "She'll do,"

she said at last. "What do I owe you?"

As Suzi rang up the till for Mrs Lockett, Bella found Sasha's collar and lead and clipped them on.

"See you again soon!" Bella said politely as Mrs Lockett swept out of the salon.

"Perhaps," said Mrs Lockett over her shoulder. "Come now, Sashikins!"

When Mrs Lockett was out of sight, Amber

brought Silky back into the salon. She put the bichon frise on the top step leading up to the bathtub.

"Your turn, Silky," Suzi sighed, and picked up the little dog.

Then she frowned. She felt Silky's belly, sniffed her fur and frowned again.

"Bella?" she said. "Are you quite sure this is Silky?"

"Oh yes," said Bella, closing the door behind Mrs Lockett. "Sasha's head smelled of lavender shampoo, so I knew it was Sasha."

Suzi had a funny look on her face. "This dog already looks and smells freshly washed to me," she said. She sniffed Silky's head. "And she

smells of lavender shampoo too."

Bella's stomach swooped. "That's impossible!" she said. "Isn't it?"

She turned to Amber, hoping she might be able to shed some light on the situation. It was her detective skill after all that had helped them find Pepper when he went missing. Perhaps she could solve this mystery too.

"Hmmm," Amber muttered, deep in thought. "I went to hide in the flat with Sasha when Mr Boswell came in, but I couldn't help peeking from behind the door to see what was going on."

Suzi raised her eyebrows, but Amber went on, "Didn't Mr Boswell stroke Silky after he picked up the shampoo?"

Bella nodded.

"Well, his fingers had shampoo on them and would have smelled of lavender!" Amber paused and then added dramatically, "So then Silky's head would have smelled of lavender too. No wonder Bella got the dogs mixed up!"

Suzi clutched her head. "Oh," she moaned. "*We've given Mrs Lockett the wrong dog!*"

Five

Swapsies

"Should we chase after Mrs Lockett and explain
the mix-up?" said Bella as everyone stared at
Sasha.

"No!" Suzi rubbed her eyes, like she always
did when she was trying to think. "She'll be
furious! Switching dogs? It's a nightmare!"

Bella felt terrible. Louie and Joe came downstairs to see what all the fuss was about.

"Oh boy," said Joe, grinning as Amber explained what had happened. "You are in serious trouble."

"We know," Bella muttered.

"Hee hee hee!" Louie squealed.

"Stop laughing, Louie," Bella added crossly. "It's not very helpful."

Louie stopped.

"Well," said Suzi gloomily. "No point in washing you again, Sasha."

Sasha gave a tiny bark of agreement and sat down on her curly white bottom.

Bella knew it was up to her to think of

something. She was the one who'd got the dogs the wrong way round. She thought hard.

"Mrs Lockett thought Silky was Sasha," she said slowly. "Now we have to persuade Mr Boswell that Sasha is Silky. Then we can swap the dogs back again at the show tonight."

Louie and Joe both started laughing again. Suzi looked sick. Even Pepper stopped crunching on his bone for a minute.

"Impossible, Bella!" Amber said, shaking her head. "You might fool Mr Boswell when he picks Sasha up. But Mrs Lockett and Mr Boswell will watch each other like hawks during the show. I think they'd notice if we marched up and swapped their dogs round!"

"The judges and all the people at the show would notice too," Louie said.

Bella looked at the floor, wondering how they could distract everyone at the show so they could make the switch. Sasha panted patiently, her little pink tongue peeping out of her mouth.

"OK," said Suzi, sitting down. "*Now* I'm panicking."

Over in his basket, Pepper had started eating his bone again.

"I wish you'd take that stinky thing out in the yard, Pepper," Suzi grumbled.

"Woof!" said Pepper.

Sasha trotted down the steps of the bathtub

and went over to sniff the bone. Pepper
growled. Sasha yapped, and sat down a safe
distance away.

Watching the two dogs gave Bella an idea.
The more she thought about it, the more she
believed it could work.

"I know what we can do!" she said.
"Listen..."

Half an hour later, the salon door tinkled.

"Is Silky ready?" Brian Boswell said, striding

inside and shutting the door behind him.

"You've had plenty of time. I hope you've done

a good job, because there's no time left to

correct any mistakes."

Sitting in the window seat with Amber beside

her and Pepper on her knee, Bella watched

as her mum picked up Sasha. Suzi held the

bichon frise out to Mr Boswell. Bella hoped

Mr Boswell couldn't see her mum's hands

trembling.

Mr Boswell checked the white fur under

Sasha's eyes for tearstains and sniffed her coat. He stroked her curly fur and fluffed her ears.

"She's a different dog," he said at last.

Bella couldn't help it. A gasp escaped from her lips. Giving Amber an agonised look, she almost missed Mr Boswell's next words.

"It's amazing what a wash and blowdry can do," said Silky's owner. "I hardly recognise her. You've done a good job."

He held Sasha up to his face. Sasha put out her little tongue and licked him on the nose, but

Bella could have sworn there was a look
of mild confusion in the little dog's shiny black
eyes.

"Clever little Silky-pops," Mr Boswell cooed,
nuzzling the little dog. "You know your daddy,
don't you? Come along now. We've got a show
to win."

The relief made Bella feel faint. They'd done
it! Amber gave her a silent thumbs-up and
winked. Thank goodness her mum had banished
the boys upstairs. They would have given the
game away for sure!

"Twenty pounds, I believe?" said Mr Boswell,
pulling out his wallet. "And here's an extra five
for your trouble."

Bella put Pepper down. She took the money and rang up the till the way her mum had shown her.

"Good luck tonight!" said Suzi brightly, opening the door to let Mr Boswell and Sasha out. "We'll see you there! We've entered Pepper, our dog, you see."

"Really?" said Mr Boswell disbelievingly. He eyed Pepper, who was scratching himself. "Whatever for?"

"Most Obedient Dog," Bella said, grinning. She was too relieved that Part One of their plan had worked to feel cross at Mr Boswell's tone of voice, or worried about whether Pepper would behave himself tonight.

"Oh yes," said Mr Boswell with a sniff. "I hear they aren't very particular about that group."

And with those words, he was gone, holding Sasha firmly in his arms.

"Oh my goodness gracious gravy boats," said Suzi, leaning her head against the door as it tinkled shut. "I can't believe we just did that. I must be mad."

"Now all we have to worry about is Part

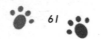

61

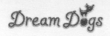

Two of our plan, Mum," Bella said. "And I have

that under control." She looked down at

Pepper. "Beg!" she ordered, like she'd seen Miss

Waldicott do with Angus the Westie.

Pepper rolled on to his back and waved his

legs in the air, asking for his tummy to be

scratched.

"And the prize for the Silliest Dog goes to..." said Amber in a grand, judge-like voice.

Bella scratched her head. She'd have to think of something that Pepper could do for the judges, or they didn't stand a chance of winning *anything*.

Louie put his head round the flat door. "Can me and Joe come down now?" he said, sounding grumpy.

"Of course," said Suzi, spreading out her arms. "As long as you are prepared to help us wash Pepper. He might not win Most Obedient Dog, but at least he'll smell nice."

"Woof!" said Pepper, bicycling his back legs as Bella and Amber both gave his tummy a good rub.

Six

Cuddles

At five minutes to seven, Bella helped her mum put Pepper into the back of their mini van. Like most of the things Suzi owned, the mini van was pink. She'd even had the Dream Dogs logo painted on the side. Bella loved it.

"Sit," Bella ordered, as Pepper dashed from

64

one side of the mini van to the other. "Pepper? Pepper! Sit!"

Pepper chased his tail with excitement. Then he flopped down with a woof.

"He did what I told him!" said Bella in triumph. "He's going to be fine."

"Maybe he *will* win the Most Obedient Dog class," said Amber.

"I think he fell over," Louie said. "I get like that when I run round in circles."

Suzi made sure everyone was strapped in. She got into the driving seat and started the engine. "We've only got four minutes to get there," she said, sounding a bit hysterical. "Thank goodness it's only round the corner."

Bella rolled her eyes at Amber as Suzi pulled away from the kerb. Her mum was always late for *everything*. Clutching tightly on to the plastic bag on her lap, Bella thought about Part Two of their plan to switch Sasha and Silky back.

"Have you got the stickers?" she said, turning to Amber.

Amber nodded. "I still think your plan's mad," she said.

"I know," said Bella, gripping her plastic bag. "But we've got to try it."

By the time they had parked at the hall, clipped on Pepper's lead and found the front door, it was ten past seven.

"Claire will kill me if we're late for Snowy's

class," Suzi panted. "Come on, kids. I think it's this way..."

The hall was warm and full of loud chatter. Bella sniffed the air. The smell of warm, woolly dogs was everywhere. Stands selling dog collars, dog food and dog toys were ranged around the walls. Owners stood in groups, drinking wine and orange juice. Their dogs were all barking at each other like mad. Bella could hardly hear herself think.

"It's crazy in here!" Amber said.

Bella stared around the room. Big yellow banners hung off the ceiling. They said things like "Pedigree Group" and "Coat in the Best Condition" and "Best Puppy". The one that

made Bella laugh was "Dog with the Waggiest

Tail". She glanced down at Pepper. His tail was

a blur.

"We should have entered Pepper for that one, Mum," she shouted, pointing out the banner to Suzi.

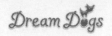

"There are lots of things we should have done," Suzi said, gazing around the room anxiously. "Like not swapping Mrs Lockett and Mr Boswell's dogs round. I really hope your plan is going to work."

Bella checked that she still had her plastic bag. It contained her Secret Weapon. "It'll all be fine, Mum," she said, trying to sound confident. "Promise."

"Hmm," said Suzi, looking unconvinced. She glanced around the room again. "Ooh, there she is," she said with relief, spotting Amber's mum. "Claire! Over here!"

Amber's mum pushed through the crowd. Snowy was beside her on his lead. "We haven't missed Snowy's class, have we?" Suzi asked as Bella stroked Snowy's shining black ears.

Claire shook her head. "They always start us a bit later than the rest of the groups," she said. "The pedigree owners are all over there, look."

Standing under the "Pedigree group" banner, Bella could see several snooty-looking owners ignoring the rest of the cheerful crowd. Most of them had brushes in their hands and were grooming their dogs. Bella could see Mr Boswell's big face rising out of the group like a round red sun. On the far side, she thought she could see Mrs Lockett.

"So, how did you get on with Mr Boswell

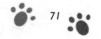

71

and Mrs Lockett, then?" asked Claire cheerfully.

Suzi cleared her throat. "We had a problem," she said. And she told Claire what had happened.

Claire put her hand to her throat. "That's terrible!" she gasped. "And they haven't *noticed*?"

Bella shook her head.

"Bella has a plan to switch them back," said Amber.

Before Bella could explain what the plan was, someone coughed into a microphone.

"Hello... Hello?" said a large, curly-haired lady on the stage. "Is this on…? It is? Ladies and gentlemen, as Mayor of Sandmouth, it is my great pleasure to welcome you all to the

Sandmouth Annual Dog Show!"

There was some loud clapping. Someone barked at the back of the hall, making several real dogs bark back.

"Will contestants please make their way to their chosen groups," said the Mayor, raising her voice over the laughter.

Bella's heart thumped as she caught sight of the "Most Obedient Dog" group at the back of the hall. "That's us over there," she said. "Let's go!"

Suzi glanced at the plastic bag in Bella's hands. "I thought we were going to sort out Sasha and Silky first?" she said, looking worried.

Bella shook her head. "Claire said they did the pedigrees a bit later, Mum," she said. "This is Pepper's big chance. Come on, Pepper!"

She tugged on Pepper's lead. Pepper sat down and scratched his ear.

"Heel!" Bella ordered.

Pepper yawned. Then he dragged himself along by his front paws so that his bottom skidded along the ground. Bella blushed and glanced around, hoping no one had seen.

"Hello, dears!" Miss Waldicott beamed at them as they all reached their group. Angus the Westie panted at her side. "Everything all right?"

Pepper sniffed Angus's bottom. Angus wasn't very pleased about it and growled.

"Fine, Miss Waldicott," Bella panted. "Stop it, Pepper!"

Pepper sneezed and sat down. Louie stuffed his fingers in his mouth to muffle his giggles when Bella glared at him.

The judge was a thin gentleman with a sprinkling of white hair. He finished shaking the paw of the Labrador on the far side of Angus and wrote something on his clipboard. Then he came towards them.

"Paw, Angus," said Miss Waldicott as the judge looked at her.

Angus sat up on his back legs and waved his paws. The judge nodded and wrote on his clipboard. Miss Waldicott made a fuss over Angus and gave him a treat.

Bella swallowed. Pepper was next.

"Let's see what you can do, then, Pepper," said the judge with a smile.

Bella put down the plastic bag containing the Secret Weapon. She got on to her knees. "Cuddle, Pepper," she said, and held out her arms.

Pepper didn't hesitate. He put his paws

round Bella's neck at once and rested his furry face against Bella's cheek. Cuddles were his favourite thing.

"Ahhh!" Bella heard Miss Waldicott say fondly. "Isn't that sweet?"

The judge smiled and made a note. Bella stood up. As she did so, she kicked her plastic bag by mistake. The bag fell over, spilling its contents. And Bella watched with horror as her Secret Weapon rolled away.

Seven

Barking Mad

It unwrapped itself as it went. And revealed...

Pepper's bone! The bone Bella had taken when

Pepper's back was turned earlier in the day.

The smelliest bone in the world.

Pepper recognised it at once. He barked in

delight. Pulling away from Bella, he dashed

after his bone.

"I thought you weren't getting that bone out until we saw Sasha and Silky!" Suzi gasped.

"It was an accident!" said Bella desperately. "Pepper wasn't supposed to see it. We have to catch him before he ruins the plan!"

"If you go before the judge makes his decision, you'll be disqualified," Miss Waldicott warned. "It would be such a shame!"

Pepper had got the bone. Now he was zigzagging around the hall, trying to find somewhere quiet to eat it. Bella was torn. She felt sure Pepper was in with a chance of winning the Obedience class rosette, the judge had been so impressed by the cuddle! But she

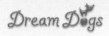

couldn't risk it. If they couldn't use the bone to tempt Sasha and Silky away from Mrs Lockett and Mr Boswell and switch them round again, Dream Dogs could be ruined!

"Good luck, Miss Waldicott!" she said, wriggling free. "I hope Angus wins!"

There was a frenzy of barking. Pepper wasn't

the only dog who'd seen the bone. The Labrador who'd shaken paws with the judge broke away from its owner. A huge Newfoundland galloped after Pepper and two little dachshunds nipped at people's ankles as they tried to follow the delicious smell. Pepper raced on, the bone clamped firmly between his teeth.

Bella dodged through the crowd. Louie and
Suzi weren't far behind.

"Excuse me... Sorry!" Bella shouted. "Excuse
me... Thanks... PEPPER!"

Pepper raced on. They were nearing the far
side of the hall now. At least six dogs were
chasing Pepper and the bone as well as Bella
and her family.

"PEPPER!!" Bella yelled hopelessly.

Pepper swerved away from the stage and
headed towards the Pedigree class. Bella
caught a glimpse of Mrs Lockett's horrified
face. In a flash, she realised their plan could still
work. Dogs didn't wear collars when they were
being judged. If Amber had already put a

sticker on Sasha's tummy like they'd planned, they could still swap the dogs in the chaos. *If...*

Please let Amber have done it! Bella prayed.

Pepper charged into the Pedigree group judging ring. Snowy was used to Pepper's crazy ways, and ignored him. But every other dog in the group, including Sasha and Silky, broke away from their owners and joined in the chase.

"Sashikins!" shouted Mrs Lockett.

"Silky-pops!" bellowed Mr Boswell.

"Will the owner *please* regain control of that little brown dog!" shouted the Mayor down the microphone.

Bella pounced. But not on Pepper, who shot underneath a table and started eating his bone. She pounced instead on the two white bichon frises scampering past her as fast as their fluffy little legs could go. Feeling under their tummies, she found a little sticker.

"Got you, Sasha," she murmured.

"Sashikins!" Mrs Lockett rushed up to Bella. "You're safe!" She looked from Sasha to Silky and back again. "Sashikins?" she asked doubtfully.

"Here you are, Mrs Lockett," Bella said, and

handed over the real Sasha.

Mrs Lockett buried her nose in Sasha's fluffy white fur as Mr Boswell raced up. He snatched Silky out of Bella's arms.

"I hope this is the right dog," he said pompously. "Everyone knows that Helen Lockett would steal Silky in a heartbeat."

"You are one to talk, Boswell!" Mrs Lockett spluttered. "You'd take Sasha if I so much as *blinked*!"

"Look for yourselves," said Bella politely. "I'm sure you know your own dogs. Don't you?"

Mr Boswell held Silky up to his face. Mrs Lockett did the same with Sasha. They both

85

stared hard. Bella fought the urge to giggle.

"Hmm," said Mrs Lockett.

"Humph," said Mr Boswell.

Giving each other dirty looks, Mrs Lockett and Mr Boswell stalked back to the Pedigree class judging ring with Sasha and Silky under their arms.

"I'm sorry," Bella heard the judge say. "You left the ring before I made my judgement. You're both disqualified."

"What!" Mrs Lockett screeched.

"Impossible!" Mr Boswell shouted.

The judge frowned at the two bichon frise owners. "As the only dog who stayed in the ring, Snowy the spaniel has won this category," he said firmly. "Now if you'll excuse me, I have

a rosette to award."

Eight

And the Rosette Goes to...

"I can't believe Snowy won his category!" Claire said, gazing down at the red rosette on Snowy's collar. She looked a bit dazed.

"He deserved it," said Bella happily.

"I'm so pleased for you, Claire!" said Suzi, clapping her hands.

Snowy woofed.

"Well, *I* think Pepper should have won Most Exciting Dog," said Louie. "That dog chase was the best thing ever!"

Everyone peered under the table, where Pepper was still chewing his bone. There wasn't much left.

"Shame they didn't have that category," Bella agreed, helping herself to some crisps. She was feeling so pleased that they'd sorted out the Sasha / Silky mix-up that she didn't really mind not winning anything.

"I still think it's strange that Mrs Lockett and Mr Boswell didn't notice that they had the wrong dogs," said Claire.

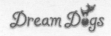

"Maybe they *did* notice," Amber suggested.

"Maybe Mrs Lockett wanted Silky and Mr

Boswell wanted Sasha all along."

"We spoiled their plans, then, didn't we?"

said Bella cheerfully. She couldn't imagine

wanting to swap Pepper for another dog. Even

if he did do embarrassing things like bottom

skids.

"I'm not sorry Mrs Lockett and Mr Boswell have left," Suzi said as she sipped her drink and looked around the room. "They weren't very nice, were they?"

"But Sasha and Silky were *adorable*," said Bella wistfully, thinking of Silky's bright eyes and Sasha's tiny pink tongue.

Up on the stage, the Mayor coughed into the microphone. Everyone stopped chattering and turned to face her.

"Another wonderful evening, I'm sure you'll all agree!" said the Mayor. "Some lovely dogs and plenty of entertainment!"

She glanced at Pepper as she said this. Pepper had finished his bone, and cocked his head happily with his tongue hanging out.

"But we have two more rosettes to award before this evening ends," continued the Mayor. "So I'd like to hand over to Mr Bellamy, our chief judge!"

Everyone clapped except Louie, whose hands were full of crisps.

"It's Pepper's judge!" Bella exclaimed, recognising the white-haired man going up to the microphone.

"I'm pleased to announce that the winner of this year's Best in Show," said Mr Bellamy, "goes to... Snowy the spaniel!"

Claire gasped and almost dropped her wine glass.

"Mum!" Amber squealed. "Snowy won!"

Bella clapped so hard that she hurt her hands as Amber's mum and Snowy climbed on to the stage to be awarded a golden rosette.

When the noise died down, Mr Bellamy smiled again. "And now for my favourite category," he said, "The Dog the Judge Would Most Like to Take Home."

Bella could hear shouts and laughter all around the room. She turned to Amber.

"I didn't see that category," she said in confusion.

"It gets awarded at the end of every show," Amber explained. "There're no rules. It's just the judge's favourite dog."

"For a beautiful demonstration of how to hug his owner," said Mr Bellamy, "not to mention all the fun of the chase, I'm delighted to award this rosette to... Pepper."

Bella felt her jaw hit the floor. Suzi squealed and Louie shouted with surprise.

"Go!" Amber cheered, pushing Bella. "On the stage, go on!"

Bella tugged Pepper's lead. Amazingly, Pepper got to his feet and trotted after her as she climbed on to the stage. The lights dazzled her eyes, and the noise was deafening.

"Well done," said Mr Bellamy. He handed Bella a beautiful green rosette. Then he bent down to pat Pepper. "I don't suppose you'd give me a cuddle, would you, boy?" he asked Pepper.

Bella's heart burst with pride as Pepper sat up and put his paws round the judge's neck. There were more cheers.

The judge straightened up. His next words were so soft that Bella almost missed them.

"This show can be very boring sometimes,"

Mr Bellamy whispered. "But not this year. Eh,

Pepper?"

"Woof!" Pepper said, and wagged his tail

hard in agreement.

Top tips from vets!

If you would like to train your dog, check out our simple tips and maybe they'll be the star of a dog show just like Pepper!

Puppies can be easily distracted, so train them for a short time but often.

Don't confuse them - only teach one thing at a time.

Make it fun! Reward your dog when they get it right with something they like, either savoury dog treats, lots of praise or play. If you use treats remember to cut down their main meals so they don't get fat!

Find a local dog training class to get advice and have fun.

Remember - NEVER punish your dog if they don't understand you.

Did you know?

You can get special seatbelts for dogs? As Pepper travels with his family in the car, he should be safely strapped in just like them.

If you would like more information on dog training visit www.pdsa.org.uk/petprotectors

for pets in need of vets

Help PDSA by joining our Pet Protectors Club!

PDSA treats the sick and injured pets of people in need.

For kids who love pets

Members get ...

Plus a free bag!

Animal year planner

Membership badge and card

Cute stickers

Animal Antics

Just £11 a year!

Personalised fridge magnet

magazine every 2 months

Sign me up!

Fill in the form and send it with a cheque or postal order for £11 made payable to 'PDSA' to PDSA Pet Protectors, Whitechapel Way, Priorslee, Telford, Shropshire TF2 9PQ.

Name .... Date of birth ....

Address ....

....

Postcode ....

Telephone ....

Protecting your information Leading veterinary charity, PDSA, uses your information to manage your membership of Pet Protectors; we will never pass these details on to anyone else for marketing purposes. Occasionally we may like to send you details of local PDSA events and activities. If you do not want us to do this, please tick this box. ☐

Registered charity nos. 208217 & SC037585

DD_Pepper_2010

Join online www.youngpdsa.org.uk or join by phone on 0800 019 9144

Dream Dogs

NUGGET

Bella and her little brother Louie are out walking their dog, Pepper, when they find a 'mud monster' stuck in a ditch!

When Bella and Louie realise that the 'monster' is a dog in distress, they bring the poor pooch back to the Dream Dogs grooming parlour. But they get a big surprise when they discover what's under all that mud...

Read on for a sneak preview of the next Dream Dogs adventure...

Mud Monster

"Over here, Louie!" Bella shouted.

Across Chestnut Park, Bella's little brother bent back his arm to throw the ball. Bella ran backwards, reaching up with her hands. Suddenly, she stumbled and toppled over, landing on her bottom. The ball sailed over her head.

"Get off!" Bella spluttered, laughing as her little dog Pepper put his paws round her neck and tried to lick her face. "Your breath stinks!"

Louie jogged over. "It's not his breath," he said. "Pepper's rolled in something smelly."

"Yuck!" Bella wrinkled her nose and pushed Pepper off. She loved Pepper, but not when he rolled in things.

"You looked funny," Louie sniggered. "Landing on your bum like that!"

"It was a bad throw," Bella told him. She got up and brushed down her jeans. "How was I supposed to catch it?"

"Haven't you ever heard of jumping?" Louie asked. "Oh, I forgot. Girls can't jump."

"Come back here and say that again!"

Bella chased Louie, laughing. Barking with excitement, Pepper followed her.

Chestnut Park was shaped like a large triangle. On one side were the backs of the shops and houses on the street where Bella and Louie lived. On another side was a busy road that Bella and Louis knew not to play near. The third side was row of much bigger houses, with large gardens and high hedges separated from the park by a stretch of woodland. Pepper loved the woods. Bella guessed that was where he'd found the stinky stuff to roll in.

Louie was running towards the trees. It was downhill part of the way. Bella ran faster, determined to catch him. At the last minute, Louie swerved. Bella couldn't stop. She toppled into the straggly ditch that separated the woods from Chestnut Park. There was a nasty squelch as she sank into the thick brown mud. Somewhere out of sight, she could hear Louie laughing like a hyena.

"That is so gross!" Bella squealed, staring in dismay at the gunge on her knees and arms.

Pepper put his head through the tall grass on the top of the ditch. One of his ears pricked up and he started barking wildly.

"Be quiet, Pepper," Bella grumbled, trying to rub the dirt off.

Pepper barked again, running up and down. His eyes were fixed on something near Bella. Bella saw what looked like a large lump of mud lying in the ditch. The lump got on to four legs and waved a long mucky tail at her.

"Louie, come quickly!" Bella shouted.

Louie's eyes almost popped out of his head. "It's a mud monster!" he shouted.

"Woof!" Pepper barked, almost beside himself.

"Don't be silly," said Bella. "It's a *dog*. The poor thing must have fallen in the ditch and it couldn't get out again!"

The dog was so caked in mud that it was having trouble opening its eyes. Louie kept a safe distance as Bella cautiously reached out her hand. The dog sniffed her fingers.

"Steady now," said Bella gently. "I'm not going to hurt you."

The dog's tail waved again. It was breathing

quite fast, like it was in shock. Bella climbed up the bank. The dog tried to follow, but scrabbled and slid back down. It wasn't wearing a collar. Bella reached down and grabbed its muddy scruff. It was a big dog, and it was heavy. She wasn't sure she could pull it out. But she was determined to try.

The dog panted hard. Its sides were heaving. Bella dug her heels in and pulled. Scrabbling and whining, the dog tried to climb the bank again. This time, it succeeded. It jumped clumsily up at Bella and licked her. This made Bella even muddier, but she didn't care.

Pepper growled and hid behind Louie as the exhausted dog flopped down on the grass. Bella looked around for the dog's owner. Apart from her and Louie, there was no one else in Chestnut Park.

"Where did it come from?" Louie asked, coming a little closer.

"Mud Monster Land," said Bella, rolling her eyes. "Oh, and thanks for all your help. I couldn't have done it without you."

"I didn't know it was a dog, did I?" Louie muttered. "It looked scary."

"Let's take it back to Mum," said Bella. "We can wash it at Dream Dogs."

She felt a little skip in her stomach at the thought of her mum's dog parlour. Dream Dogs was Bella's favourite place, with its pink walls and hanging plants and the smell of wet dog in the air. Washing the muck off to find out what kind of dog they'd found would be really exciting.

"Mum won't let you wash it in Dream Dogs," Louie said. "It's too dirty."

"That's what Dream Dogs is *for*," Bella pointed out. "Washing dogs. Remember?"

Bella teased Louie about mud monsters all the way back across Chestnut Patch. The strange dog followed Bella adoringly. Pepper pressed himself close to Louie's heels and growled every few steps.

"Pepper still thinks it's a monster," Louie said as they turned into their street.

"He's just jealous," Bella said.

It did look like Pepper was jealous. As soon as Bella unlatched the dog gate between the door of Dream Dogs and the parlour, he trotted to his basket and lay down with his back to Bella.

"Mum!" Bella said. "You'll never guess what we found!"

Bella and Louie's mum Suzi looked up from where she was drying a little white West Highland terrier. Her eyes widened.

"It's a dog," said Bella proudly.

"Take it out before it—" Suzi began.

The rest of her words were lost as the muddy dog shook itself. Bella shrieked. Louie yelled. Suzi ducked. And mud went *everywhere*.

Take home all of the
Dream Dogs
If you have it, tick it!

Available now:

PEPPER

Aimee Harper

SASHA

Aimee Harper

 ✓

Out in May:

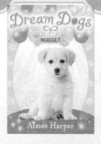

NUGGET

Aimee Harper

 ✓

CRYSTAL

Aimee Harper

Out in July:

CHARLIE

Aimee Harper

POPPY

Aimee Harper